THE
SCROOGE
OF
BITCOIN

A CHRISTMAS TALE

PAUL W. SAMUELSON

M amie Simon hated Bitcoin. There was no doubt about it.

Day after day the rich and wicked old woman sat on a large throne at the top of her Gotham City tower surrounded by her precious gold sacks and dozens of money-grubbing minions huddled at her feet. From her high and powerful seat in the chamber she plotted sinister acts against Bitcoin, constantly brooding over it, then yelling in wild fits of derangement:

"Bitcoin is a fraud! A Ponzi! A long-dead experiment!"

Indeed, Bitcoin presented a most-troubling problem for her and her large investment bank. She was often seen wringing her thin, bony hands in anguish because of the digital currency. Its design and popularity threatened her elitist power and old-money ways as it promised great hope to the world for freedom and prosperity.

"Minions!" Mamie Simon declared early on the day before Christmas, the very moment our story begins. From the great height of her throne—an elaborate red-cushioned chair trimmed in gold and rubies—she looked down at the dour underlings as they frantically jockeyed to be near her. "Minions, rub my dry, cracked feet, then go make me more money," she demanded. "I *must* find a way to destroy Bitcoin."

She laughed in a graceless, grating cackle. As she did, her rotted teeth showed brown and yellow. Her creased and painted face was equally grotesque—sallow and deathly. And her two icy blue eyes, deep in their sockets, glared coldly at everything she looked upon. Making it worse, the heavy bags under her unfeeling eyes were plump with old, purple blood. In short, she was beyond ripe. The only redeeming features in her appearance, if they could be called such at all, were the colorful flowing gown she wore and the green feather boa draped around her tall, withered neck, all of it beneath a stylish and gleaming silver hair-do.

As she now lounged back on her throne, occasionally spraying expensive perfume into the air over her narrow shoulders and drinking from an ornate goblet at her side as the minions did their work, Mamie Sloan stroked the thin skin of her chin in deep thought—and gazed slowly around the dim, circular room.

The place was a barren stone and concrete chamber. It had a tall pointed ceiling ringed high above by crouching stone gargoyles—smaller versions of the grimacing stone gargoyles on the outside of the building which leered silently over the city. There was a lifeless black-sooted fireplace with several ancient, half-burnt logs on the grate. Fat wads of paper money were stuffed carelessly here and there into the nooks and crannies of the throne. Metal coins of all sorts overflowed from several large pots and penny jars placed on either side of the tall chair. And above it all, a small, dimly lit chandelier on the end of a heavy chain hung down from the tall pointed spire.

Elsewhere, however, not a single Christmas tree or Christmas decoration could be found anywhere. There were no colorful lights or shiny garlands to celebrate the season. There were no red and white candy canes anywhere or green mistletoes hanging over the doorway or stockings on the mantle. There were no bright manger scenes or wreaths adorned in holly or Christmas cards freshly arrived in the mail. There was not even a note of Christmas music to lift the spirits. The place held no comforts of the season at all. The thick-walled chamber was filled to the brim with only cold emptiness, for in winter the cold is cheap.

And all of this was exactly how the proprietor liked it.

The current state of affairs was just as it had been, in fact, when Mamie Simon's long-dead partner, J.P. Morgue, conducted the business with her for so many years from his own gigantic throne at the center of the chamber. They had started in a small countinghouse on a dark, narrow backstreet and soon stole their way to shining world prominence. Even among greedy bankers the two of them were known as greedy bankers— happiest and most agreeable when their fingers were in somebody else's wallet. But J.P. Morgue had died unceremoniously of a weak spine and bad intentions and had taken a final tight-fisted ride with the undertaker on this very day seven years before. So the banking firm known as *Simon & Morgue, Ltd.*—the rusted name still displayed on the outside of the imposing tower for all of the city to see, the whole ominous structure silhouetted against the sky like a sword against God—became hers and hers alone. Not for a single moment did Mamie Simon miss her old, overfed business partner and his dramatic baleen mustache. And she answered to the business in her own way.

The chamber at the top of the tower had only one small window. Like every day, crouched at a little table next to the window in a tiny square of morning sunlight, sat Mamie Simon's chief clerk and best employee. Even though he had been a faithful servant to her for many years, her eyes set upon the innocent man and glowered at him fiercely:

"Bob Cratchit!" she screeched at the bent figure. "Come here and massage my jowls. Then recite to me how much fiat I hold in my coffers."

Bob Cratchit, wearing a threadbare coat, ragged old sweater, and fingerless gloves in the chamber's dank air, sat hunched over a pile of ledger books in which he worked his fingers raw adding and subtracting rows and columns of bankers' numbers. The scroungy-looking man, upon his arrival at work that day, had said "Good morning!" to his boss as he lightly passed by her—he had been in quite high spirits, as it was, and he did not feel a need to creep into work submissively as was so often the case—but these were her very first words to him.

Hearing the unpleasant words in their unpleasant tone, he slowly raised his head to her, brushing aside his neglected, overgrown hair which fell over his eyes and covered his long sideburns. He was suddenly no longer in quite so lofty a mood. Only a moment earlier he had joyfully and longingly looked out the window where the bright, snow-covered streets far below bustled with Christmas shoppers among the neon skyscrapers and merry-makers in the festooned bars and restaurants saying "Happy Yuletides!" to one another over cans of grog. Through the thin glass pane—envisioning himself strolling among those happy, well-lit crowds—a hint of laughter and cheerful Christmas music had even faintly made it to his ears amid the distant ringing of church bells.

Now, though, the air in the room was filled with the old lady's disturbing voice. Her meanness showed through her every syllable as if there was an incurable boil swelling in her personality.

Upon hearing his name, the pleased, faraway look in Bob Cratchit's eyes quickly changed to fright . . . then disgust . . . then defiance as he turned and peered at the shriveled figure on the throne. Her appearance was no more inviting and forgiving than a bleached whalebone. He visibly shivered that his God-given moniker had traveled over her stale tongue and through the chasm of her ghoulish mouth, and he looked upon her with contempt.

This would be the moment, he decided, to speak his mind—all of his mind—as difficult as it would be and as forbidden as it was. She had pushed him into a veritable corner and he would not wait another second, for he had something to say:

"Mamie Simon," he stated with deliberation from his personal Tank next to the window. "For years I have worked at the foot of your throne putting up with your wild rantings and pilfering directives. I am now ashamed to say I simply grew accustomed to them all." He grimaced in self-condemnation. "Even so," he continued, "ever since moving away from London to take this cheerless banking position I have never said anything against you or your banking and investment business. I have kept my mind at a distance, at no time letting the firm of Simon & Morgue, Ltd. weigh on my conscience. But, now, as of today, I have made a final decision about my future. I can put it off no longer."

Mamie Simon's eyes widened in surprise that the contorted shape huddled in the square of light was talking without being told.

"Bah, Cratchit! You've been thinking?" the high-handed woman said. "And now you're *talking*? Insufferable! What right have you to think and speak on my time? I don't pay you for such menial things when there's no profit in it to be seen." She growled to herself, then with a mighty scowl she clenched her teeth, speaking through her lips. "You are the Overlooked Man, Cratchit, a mere mug in the mob. You have no choice in any matter and that's the way it will stay because the world doesn't know you. But I do! So I will tell you what to think when I want you to think, do you hear, *servant*? Until that time, lay down your pencil and *commence on my jowls.*"

A mild-mannered and agreeable man, congenial and warm, Bob Cratchit had always been an obedient steward of the business doing whatever his boss commanded of him from her sovereign chair. He'd rarely seen her depart from the chair, in fact. It was from that high and dignified location she hatched all of her greedy schemes against the world that ruined so many lives while adding millions in profits to her own.

But now Bob Cratchit shook his head at her slowly, indicating he would not obey her command. He had reached his limit. There would be no more of such ungodly work while reading off her balance sheets and income statements or fawning over her annual reports. He would no longer avert his eyes and give in to her pressures. He would no longer bow in subservience. He would not do any of it anymore. He had never been so insolent in her presence, and his insolence continued:

"What gall have you to command anyone to do such a thing, Mamie Simon?" he asked with a slow shake of his head. Her arrogance of position was disdainful to him. "I might be overlooked by the world, but I am happy to say I have rubbed your jaw bags for the last time. You can count and stack your own fiat, too. As of this minute, I will not toil for you any longer far up in this terrible tower."

He rose from his little wooden stool at the table, a bit shakily under the circumstances, snuffing out with his fingers the small candle he used for warmth. He stood alongside the table rubbing his gloved hands over one another, working the circulation. After a pause, as the high lady looked down on him from her cruel, ruthless eyes, sneering and grinding her molars, he continued his impromptu resignation speech:

"I rebuke you entirely, Mamie Simon," he stated, still gaining his knees. "I rebuke everything about your existence and I will serve you no longer. Starting today, you can rely on your programmed Harvard and Yale and other Ivy League minions to massage those all-important jowls." He pointed towards the group of minions on the floor, all of them well-dressed and stylish in their modern dark blue suits and skirts with starched white collars and fine lapels, as they looked back at him. "Feast your eyes on those clustered figures there at the base of your throne," he went on, "fighting each other for the chance to knead and caress your precious feet—and proud to do it. Indeed, they can do your big-city banking and bidding with their shiny MBAs and fancy economics and accounting degrees. They're young and attractive with everything ahead, fresh from their indoctrinations, yet now they cower here in Satan's Nest with all of their debt for the privilege. So let them learn their lessons. As for me, I have learned mine. I am done with your feet and your fiat, Mamie Simon. I am done with your jowls and ledgers and shiny hair, too. I don't want any of it anymore. You are the Scrooge of our time, and I hereby resign myself from this dreadful situation."

Bob Cratchit, on-edge throughout this whole confrontation with his long-time boss, smiled in relief that he was able to say what he wanted to say. In fact, he had no idea he had it in himself. The words had simply flowed out in some unconscious waterfall. All at once, he felt cheerful in his heart and brawny in his outlook for, to be sure, he had done it.

Meanwhile, the purple bags under Mamie Simon's smoldering eyes quivered in her sudden shock and anger.

"Bah, *Cratchit*," she cried out, looking down her up-in-the-air nose while jabbing a long, crooked finger at him. "You're *defying* me? Defying *me*? It's an unabashed *humbug*."

"I am not some mangy dog under your dinner table," he replied.

She lurched forward in her chair, still pointing at him sternly across the room. "I *pay* you and therefore I *own* you, Cratchit. I rule the world you live in and I rule *you*. Most assuredly, you *are* a rotten dog and you'll continue begging me for the scraps I drop for you right here in this tower." She shook a veined, withered fist at him. "So, *Chief Clerk*, do as I say or I'll have you tied to these over-educated, over-priced minions and you'll be rubbing my toes till the end of time!"

Looking a bit surprised at being labeled in such ways—and who wouldn't be surprised by such blusterings?—the fresh-faced minions at her feet began to whisper and murmur among themselves.

Bob Cratchit would not back down, though. He had started something he could not go back on, and he stood tall with resolve and a moderately good spine despite his years hunched over the tiny table. He snatched his faded hat from the corner of the table and, placing it on his head, started towards Mamie Simon with a sturdy lightness in his step to face her straight-away. He moved as if he had lost some of a long-held heavy burden. Like the Ghost of Christmas Yet-to-Come, he very nearly floated above the floor.

Then, standing in front of her oddly captivating visage, he took a deep breath before speaking once again:

"My poor Mamie Simon," he stated in a strong, confident voice, gazing up at her. "Despite your constant efforts, I have recently been developing a new outlook on the world. It is one you will not like—since you like very little, anyway—and my conclusion is even a surprise to me."

She stared at him grimly. "Tut, tut, tut—is that so, Cratchit? A new *outlook*, you say? And what is your surprising con*clu*sion?" Her fingers clenched the arms of the chair as if to prevent herself from flying off into the room like a mad banshee. "What is causing this blood-raising insubordination I must put a stop to and which is costing me precious time and capital?"

"I will make it simple for you, old woman," he remarked, rubbing his hands again for warmth, still in disbelief he was talking to her like this. "My conclusion is the following: I am a free and rational man—free to do what I will and will not choose. Liberty and self-determination are my born rights. As a consequence, I will not be shackled and burdened by your measly wages and gross manipulations anymore. I will not be led around by you like I am on a tether—I am no donkey. There are better things in life than your icy death-grip around my neck, I am sure of it. So, in the spirit of Christmas and everything good, this man will go his own way. I am done entering your debits and credits and tracking your dollars and cooking your books. I am done with your over-charges and under-dealings and—"

"Bob Cratchit," she broke in with a cry. "You cannot *leave* me. You are my counting clerk and my servant and that is final. You will be here at sunrise Christmas morning and you will stay on my rolls every day afterwards because I say so. Now, get to your senses and get to my jowls."

But he was determined. "Mamie Simon, I *can* leave you, and I will. There is no stopping me. You can assign those sagging cheeks to another."

For Bob Cratchit, this glum and desolate place of business had always been more snowbank than investment bank—and he fully intended to escape its cold bite.

"Humbug!" she went on, taken aback by the turn. "Bob Cratchit you're being Bob Crotchety! What's gotten into your mealy mind today? A fever? A hemorrhage? I should bar the door and have a go at you with a switch. This outburst is entirely out of your character." She angrily grabbed a fistful of paper bills stuffed in the creases of her throne and threw them spitefully to the floor. Then she waved two dismissive hands at him, and the numerous jeweled bracelets decorating her arms clinked and jangled. "You do not know how to live in liberty, Cratchit," she continued sternly. "What is liberty to you? Adding numbers in your head? Sharpening a pencil? Sipping tea? Look at the facts of your beige, humdrum life: You need me to tell you what to do, how to do it, and when to begin. I am indispensable to your every functioning moment. You are mine, there is no question. So I will not listen to any more of this inane rubbish about born rights and going your way. Chattel does not talk back to its owner or leave on its own. Now, again . . . *serve my purposes.*"

She was an old-time, salty, contentious, miserable, stingy, unfeeling, silly, odious, powerful banker—and she acted like one. Every night she slept on an iron pillow and every day she sat on her stiff, gaudy throne throwing hard words in all directions. At present, her stinging voice reverberated in the bleak chamber penetrating the sacred core of all who heard it. Yet Bob Cratchit remained standing exactly as he was, unperturbed. There was no questioning his will.

"You will now listen to *me* for once, Mamie Simon," he demanded of her, "because everybody should know what I know, even a small-minded, billowing banker as ghastly as yourself." He took off his hat and held it at his side. "Last night, for the first time, I purchased some Bitcoin off a decentralized exchange. I am no intellectual, but I've made a study of Bitcoin, you see, despite your eternal rantings against it, and I have slowly begun to understand its vision and the new path it presents. It's an ingenious invention, far-ranging and simple at the same time—intricately layered, strong and tested, borne out of runaway passion. Yes, Mamie Simon, true and good passion, something you'll never know. All acts of passion are borne out of love or money, and Bitcoin was founded on both."

"*Bah*, not Bitcoin, Cratchit, you buffoon," she shouted. "You think you're leaving me for Bitcoin? A thousand humbugs!"

She raised both of her fists at him and feebly shook them in his direction.

"Indeed, Mamie Simon, I *am* leaving you," he replied. "Bitcoin has opened my mind to a new reality. Bitcoin has become my new stimulant, my call to adventure. It is money for the world without gatekeepers."

"Go ahead, tell yourself that!"

"I *am* telling myself. I now know with the freedom of Bitcoin *nobody* can rule me, not even a rich, miserly, soul-less matron like yourself at the top of this lonely spire."

"*Hum*bug," she grumbled. Then, with disapproval in her voice, she added more softly: "You're less dead than you appear, Cratchit."

"Well, you have no doubt helped push me into this decision, old woman," he went on confidently, "so blame yourself. Blame your tongue and your temper and your tantrums. While you bark at the ceiling every day, complaining about the world, I try my utmost to live a life of abundance despite my tiny home's meager cupboards. But even I have my limits—I have been poor enough. The House of Cratchit is in tatters. There are times I barely have two copper coins to rub together. But, now, for the first time in my life, without anybody's permission, I am an investor and a saver. Did you hear? An *investor* and a *saver!* And it's all because of Bitcoin. What more do I need? I have only put into it what little spare change I could find in my pockets. Nonetheless, I am in the game—at the tip of the spear—and I am gung-ho for the prospects. It is all only a matter of sweet time, Mamie Simon. So, for myself and my family and my poor son Tiny Tim, who is unwell and must use a crutch to get around, I must go. My tipping point of misery has been reached. I have a Bitcoin dream to follow: Only regret is on the other side of an unpursued dream and I will not have such a thing hanging over me. Therefore I am putting my faith in the future, starting today, for optimism is all I have left." He placed his hat over his heart. "I have seen the dark and the light, madam. In the world of humans, Bitcoin is a beacon showing the way."

Bob Cratchit had found his eternal guiding star—his Christmas Star, to be sure. And he was more than happy with it. He could see that Bitcoin was strong and, by proximity, making him stronger. He could feel the power of it growing in his chest every moment, even in these early days. Across the way, however, listening to this surprising and unwelcome dissertation, the old dame turned even more indignant, and she rose high in her seat.

"How *dare* you," she yelled, her craggy, bloodless face in a snarl, licking her shiny-red, overdone lips from side to side in disgust. "How dare you try to betray me,

Bob Cratchit. How dare you talk to me in such a long-winded fashion. How *dare* you even *think* for yourself." Like every day in her tower chamber, her sour breath filled the air. "Humbug to it all, Cratchit, and humbug to you," she went on, her eyes narrowing. "I hate Bitcoin and if you own Bitcoin I hate you, too."

In the past, this kind of loud and overbearing reaction would have caused Bob Cratchit to scamper back to the hard comfort of his little table, his face to be buried in the worn pages of a ledger book—his customary fender against the harsh business world. Now, however, he grinned slyly and wagged his head slowly in the way only a man sure of himself can do.

"That is my new badge of honor, isn't it, Mamie Simon?" he observed in a calm, deliberate manner. "Your hate for me—you've finally given me something I can treasure."

He regarded her silently for a moment, unafraid of her eye contact, unsettling as it was. Without a doubt, she was an adverse witness who deserved his harsh treatment. He then put his hat back on his head and slipped his thumbs through the front belt loops of his baggy woolen trousers, old and worn as they were. Bob Cratchit stood firmly and comfortably in his spot displaying his command of the situation.

"I have awoken, old lady," he continued. "You can see it plainly. I have awoken to find myself standing in the radiance of the golden coin"—he smiled a little as he said it—"and I cannot go back. As my feeble Tiny Tim said to me last night in his little voice as I tucked him into bed, 'God bless us all, father, for the Great Bitcoin will deliver us to the way the world always should be.' Yes, Mamie Simon, my young son said it just so. He is a wise boy, far wiser than his years or his father or his father's master. So I am doing something about it right now, to rectify my side of the equation."

Bob Cratchit could not unlearn what he now knew—and Tiny Tim was counting on him. The Spirit of Bitcoin had infused the man's very soul. Its all-encompassing glow was life-giving, he thought, and his mindset had transformed for the better almost overnight because of it. Bob Cratchit was with BTC and BTC was with him.

Explicit as this fact was, Mamie Simon was fully aghast at this turn of events and would not accept anything he said.

"Bah, humbug, Cratchit!" the black-hearted figure on the throne proclaimed with a sinister, throaty gurgle. "Your *Great Bitcoin* has died a thousand times and it will die a thousand more until the day it runs out of time. It is decentralized, deflationary nonsense, a fake *New Gold*, a ridiculous peer-to-peer fancy. How can such a thing's value come only from math and mining, anyway? Tell me that! You can't because there's no value behind it. Proof-of-Work, you say? I say Proof-of-Hogwash! Adam Back, you celebrate? I say Adam Backwards! Indeed, someday soon my double-spending will give you double-vision, Cratchit, then you'll understand." She scoffed at him coldly. "How silly you must be to tie your wagon to an electric coin with so little vintage. How senseless you are to chase false idols."

"Listen to me, Mamie Simon—" he started.

She would not let him speak, however, holding up to him a flat hand. Through her outrage and disgust, she chuckled darkly to herself while leaning her head back in disbelief at his folly.

"Imaginary money!" she went on derisively. "What good is money, anyway, if you can't fill your pockets with it and crinkle the bills and jingle the coins and toss a copper to a beggar?" She snickered some more. "Gold and silver and all the good metals, these are ready money. *These* can be cash in your hand and cash on the barrelhead. Think of it, Bob Cratchit. Money needs to be felt and seen and heard—a symphony to the senses. Yes, that's what it is: A grand symphony. Not some bad magic. So, again, I say to that overly soggy and boggy brain of yours, *hum*bug to it all—*humbug, humbug, humbug!*"

Filled with her own brand of stern defiance, she raised the large goblet at her side up to her mouth with two frail, trembling hands, tipping her head back and deeply drinking the dark liquid from it—all the while, between swallows, mumbling to herself about "loyalty" and Gotham City's ragged and ungracious "Bitcoin *losers* and *wisen*heimers"—as Bob Cratchit took a single step backwards preparing to withdraw from the room forever.

Material money had gotten the world to this point in history, he thought, but the current fiat system was finally breaking down—nearly everybody was losing ground. The central banks had built a finely-tuned network of institutions—a money machine—under which only they could win. Mamie Simon loved the central bankers and had joined forces with them, often praising the Cantillon Effect and so many other obscure "Effects" they produced. The central banks had always been good to Simon & Morgue's bottom line. But Bob Cratchit had witnessed first-hand that central banks are immoral, communistic entities—the evil is in the name itself—and their roughshod, inflationary ways had bred only difficulty, disparity, and destitution for ordinary folks everywhere. "We live under the serpent at our risk," he would often find himself saying, recognizing that the creeping serpent of socialism had already infiltrated and distorted and weakened so many aspects of the republic—the very aspects everybody complained of. Happily, he could see Bitcoin was now in the process of minting a new renaissance across the world— a renaissance founded on *de*centralization. The serpent supporters would strongly fight it, of course— centralization of power and control is their thing—but he foresaw that Bitcoin would destroy the lies and "herd morality" of these sickly and envious types on their drive to tyranny. Instead, Bitcoin would exult the strong. It would make everybody stronger. Bitcoin would balance the world while leading it to greater destinations.

Sadly, he seemed to be the only one in the room able to see more than a few minutes into the future.

As he stepped back, scanning the scene, he was surprised to be reminded of a time not long ago when Mamie Simon enjoyed the company of a pet rat which sat on her lap day after day—under the control of collar and leash, of course—while she petted it in slow, steady strokes and whispered her deepest secrets and desires into its tiny ears. From all appearances, she and the rat were a royal team way up there on their throne. But being subjected to all aspects of Mamie Simon's foul nature at close range day after day eventually put the rodent under high stress, which high stress resulted in the loss of its hair and appetite as well as the outer fringes of its sanity. If anybody needed the services of an unhealthy rat, this was a good one. Fortunately, the skinny, bald, beady-eyed creature of little distinction was exceptional in one way: It had superb instincts. After what must've been weeks of planning, the beaten-down, homesick rat was able to escape late one night from its high lap of misery and return to the freezing-wet city sewers far below where its life would be more agreeable and fulfilling.

Not by any design was Mamie Simon's tower the only rat-less building in Gotham City.

At present, Bob Cratchit felt like the smart rat—with a bit more distinction but the same justified lack of loyalty. He was making his break from the cold, stony chamber. It would not be long now, he thought, before he was on his way home—permanently. It had seemed like a lifetime, a dismal one. All of his memories from the place rested askew in his head like the tilting headstones in an overgrown, overpopulated cemetery. He especially wanted out before early nightfall when the darkness shrouding the tall tower would show through the window like the black cape of death.

"I'm finally tired of it all," he said to her without deference, continuing his offensive. "I'm especially tired of your never-ending humbugs, Mamie Simon. Everything to you is a humbug—it's a *bah*, then it's a *humbug*, and it never stops. But life is better than that, old lady. Indeed, where is your open-mindedness? Your flexibility of thought? Your simple goodness?"

"They're all at the bottom of this bottomless goblet," she answered in her smugness.

This was the season in Gotham City when civilization is caged inside while the Wild Animal of Winter runs unstoppable through the icy streets and canyons. A bank of ominous clouds had now rolled into the city, obscuring the sunny sky, and a sudden snowstorm started swirling outside the little window and among the skyscrapers. The clouds, which set in and blanketed the tower and dimmed the city, were the color of concrete and looked as heavy.

Such a typical Christmas Eve in Gotham!

Meanwhile, oblivious to the storm, or maybe working in concert with it, Mamie Simon put down her drink and for a moment extended both of her cold, colorless hands—attached to the ends of her long and thin cold, colorless arms—towards Bob Cratchit, grasping at the air wishing to pull him back into her fold. She reached out, her neck extended and her mouth open, her tongue probing the air. But her graspings and probings did nothing. They were not persuasive. Bob Cratchit did not move towards her at all. He simply didn't care about this frigid place anymore, or about this frigid woman, and he wanted to leave no matter the weather or anything else. Then, after a few agonizing seconds, unrewarded by her contortions and probings and strange gesticulations, Mamie Simon slowly retreated into the shadows of her high and protective chair. Her ashen hands retracted, also, and gently started stroking the long, green feather boa hanging loosely from her neck as if it was a comforting companion.

"Hear me now, Cratchit," she next said in a low raspy voice, bringing herself to attention. In the changing light, her face went from green to blue to gray. "Humbugs to the side, don't waste what little treasure you have on some baseless, invisible currency. Hear me! You mustn't be dumber than you already are, a poor oaf with no goose on his table," She paused, expecting her counterpart to have something to say at this point, to intervene and argue the insult—perhaps to agree with her? Or to sing the merits of goose-less meals?—but rather he said nothing. So she sneered on. "You see, I have studied Bitcoin, too, Cratchit. I have studied it all . . . Szabo and Finney and the whole gang, all of those money-meddlers from years ago. The white paper, the algorithms, the mysteries of its creation, all the talk of Austrian economics and this and that and the other. Theory and fantasy, all of it. Who cares about Rothbard and Mises, anyway? Or even old laissez-faire Adam Smith? Who really cares about thinkers like them? They aren't here now." She leaned forward, grinding her teeth slowly as she smirked directly at his face. "So, I have concluded once and for all—and listen to me carefully, Bob Cratchit—Bitcoin is all of *nothing* . . . nothing but bits and coins, coins and bits. A complete humbug. What could it ever be but electronic foolery? *What could it ever be?*"

Bob Cratchit shook his head again in melancholy. A primitive mind needs an adversary, he thought. This limited boss of his, this unknowable woman with no background—or one nobody wanted to think of—was telling herself wrong things and trying to bully both him and Bitcoin as a result. But it was not to be. Lies are weak and illusions are fake, and both he and Bitcoin were far too strong as adversaries. At the same time, she seemed to be clawing at the idea of an understanding, still far away despite her studies, yet Bob Cratchit knew it would never come. Shallow curiosity wrapped in knee-jerk disdain surely was not enough.

Her hands again momentarily reached forward in his direction—desperately—her fingers working against emptiness as she awaited his reply. He cooly looked into her eyes at the same time, those fierce, frenetic blue eyes far back in their caves, and he wondered what dastardly thoughts were brewing behind them—as what might brew in a witch's pot.

Mamie Simon had a daughter, it should be noted, who had visited Simon & Morgue's forbidding tower in the clouds from time to time in the past. Bob Cratchit had once overheard this daughter—a surprisingly attractive and sensible young woman—whisper excitedly to another that "on a dare" she had purchased a couple of Bitcoins for herself. In fact, this was the first time Bob Cratchit had ever heard the word "Bitcoin."

He now recounted this fact to Mamie Simon, that even her own blood owned some Bitcoins.

"My *daughter*," Mamie Simon replied, "is a misfit. She's a chronic freethinker who saves her money and invests it when she could be controlling *the whole money system* from on-high with me. Do you understand, Cratchit? Humbug to her! Who wouldn't want to join me on this comfortable throne? But, *no*— she won't do it. She says it's immoral, what I do. She says she's busy with other things that interest her. She even has a number of *friends* in her life and a so-called *respectable* job, the brazen freak. She's not daughter enough to me—not a bar-sinister, but just the same—so I have banned her from this tower. And believe my words, Cratchit, I will handle her in my own way when the time comes. It will *not* be pleasant."

Hearing this, Bob Cratchit was practically beside himself with sudden anger and concern. This was a level of wretchedness he had never seen.

"You will destroy your own daughter for owning a few Bitcoins?" he asked.

"If I must."

"Weren't you ever a young lady far in the past, holding big dreams inside a warm heart?"

"*Bah! Never*, Cratchit! I don't recall such a time and I don't care if I ever do."

"For the sake of Our Lord, and for the sake of family and affection," he went on, "I wish I could make you understand, Mamie Simon. You should be proud of that wonderful young lady—she is not some dreadful worm in the dirt. She only wants to live her life in the way she sees fit, as an upstanding individual, minding her own business and making the world a little better by being a little better herself. She has a glowing future, Bitcoin or not." His face then darkened and his voice deepened. "But nothing about your autocratic ways surprises me anymore, you sad wretch. All the years I've worked for you, you've been full of the crud. Every day in this place is a decade in the Dark Ages. Yet this is the lowest I've seen you go. Indeed, old lady, you stink and you smell and you think like a devil. You've got the empty imagination of a central banker and the barren life of one, too. Those are among your tragedies—"

"Ha, ha, Cratchit. For once you may be right," she snickered in an uneasy, forced way, not wanting to hear anymore, trying to deflect his truthful words. But the interruption only made her look worse.

"And that is why I *must* leave you," he continued. "If you understood Bitcoin as a Force to the Good, and if you were good-hearted about it yourself, you would see the great possibilities. You could be a shining hero to many, not the stylish demon you are. But you and your Park Avenue elites are long on money and short on sense—indeed, money begets money and nonsense begets nonsense. You take and take from the people and direct them how to think and live from your secret lairs in the clouds, pulling strings like puppet masters, looting their precious savings as they pinch and scratch to make good and decent lives. You pillage and then you pillage some more, never looking into the faces of those who bear your results, all the while throwing shimmering penthouse parties high above the smoking sewers and greasy streets." He felt a sudden and additional degree of warmth in his body against the friction of this moment. "For certain, Mamie Simon, you and your glowing friends think you're being clever. But I'm proud to say *my* people, the *grungy masses* to you, have awoken to your evil doings: Your banks and corporations and governments that have formed a web of cabals to conspire against the well-being of the world. The thievery, the secret dealings, the invasions, the censorships, the propagandist ad agencies following the script, the brainwashings of the young, the scare tactics, the taxes and fees and regulations, devaluing our money without due process or any recourse at all—it's nothing but scam after scam." As he spoke to her, Bob Cratchit grew angry, then angrier, realizing once more to himself how much the world had decayed under the cabals. Then he added sternly: "It has been a great time in history for you and your globalist bureaucrats and moneycrats and all the other evilcrats. What a shameful bunch you are—*each* of you." He poked a serious finger in her direction. "Yes, you're a demon, Mamie Simon, a despicable demon in pretty clothes!"

Bob Cratchit paused for a moment, practically out of breath, his mind in a rush at the things he was saying. Of course, he knew his words and ideas went against the globalist narrative and that the globalist cult would be eager to suppress him. So he glanced over his shoulder. He half-expected a grave central banker to knock on the chamber's door, step inside, and say to him like a dictator, "*Take what you get!*"

As for Mamie Simon herself, she was hardly fazed by anything he said. She was a banker—an honored and protected class. She knew that she and the cabals and all of the other bankers were always safe, they could do whatever they wanted whenever they wanted—their high parties would go on—for in such a liberal world none of their dreadful dealings and criminal stealings would ever be hangable offenses.

A quiet pause had fallen over the room at this instant. In the drafty air, the chandelier hanging above the elaborate throne swung ever-so-slightly and noticeably on its long, creaky chain. . . .

Bob Cratchit was often accustomed to glancing toward the window, no matter the circumstance, as it was the only source of true light in the chamber. As he did so at this moment, a colossal black figure appeared just beyond it. He was surprised, for it was as if the whole window suddenly became covered in the wings of a dark, menacing shadow. But it wasn't a shadow at all. Instead, the figure took the shape of the largest raven he had ever seen, and it landed on the stone windowsill outside.

The shadowy, beady-eyed new arrival glared without feeling into the chamber through the frosty glass. "Oh, look at the pretty birdie," Mamie Simon cheered and clapped at its appearance. The enormous raven's eyes, however, like two shiny black moons, moved darkly to look at Bob Cratchit himself. The man merely stared back—a bit taken aback at such an ominous visitor, but steely—and he wondered why such a creature wasn't out harassing some pigeons or standing tall on a stone owl's head. Nonetheless, the two gazed at each other, motionless, as if to determine a winner. Clearly, even during the most joyous times of the year dark forces from the outside may come intruding! After another minute, to his delight, the menacing bird framed at the window blinked, squawked loudly through the glass to voice its disapproval of the man, and took flight from the windowsill vanishing into the snowy streets below.

Such an occurrence!

The scruffy, passionate character in league with Bitcoin turned back to Mamie Simon. She was angry he had made the pretty bird fly away, and her already silent and sinister expression towards him became even grimmer—like the raven's. Yet Bob Cratchit was not afraid, even if the world and its birds and its old ladies and all of the signs of gloom were against him—and he was able to focus and continue. One cannot be sinister without sin, and he knew the power of Good is always strongest. For sure, he had more to say to her and he wanted to speak all of his mind while he could, his feelings about so many of these things having been pent-up and ready to come out for so long.

"We trusted you and your ilk for years," he continued in stark determination. "But now we know all of you lying, stealing conspirators leading the world on a downward drift are Marxist devils—the godless and the guilty. You heard me right, Mamie Simon! The light has been turned on you totalitarian monsters, you loons with your goons. You don't care about liberty for the individual—about individuals at all—and your time is coming up."

Being so confronted, and beginning to take his blusterings more seriously, the old woman's upper lip curled into a sneer.

"How *dare* you take this tone with me, Cratchit," she said as if she had any real power over his mind any longer, or as if saying such a thing was a strong retort. "I might be godless and I might be guilty. I might even be a little Marxie devil. But you wait and see. I'll put heavy chains on Bitcoin. I'll watch it wilt and die like a forsaken poinsettia. Soon, there will be only me and the clanks and rattlings of the Ghost of Bitcoin Past, and together we will haunt you forever, wherever you may go."

Her laugh echoed throughout the cold, hard expanse.

"Mercy upon you, Mamie Simon," he replied with an annoyed shake of his head. "You are excellent at destroying things, it is in your nature, but you should understand by now Bitcoin's ledger is battle-hardened and secure and you are a consensus of only one. The inertia towards its destiny is set. So stop it all—stop in your tracks right here—your plots of destruction are meaningless."

For Bob Cratchit, this whole disconcerting event in the chamber had turned into a sort of catharsis. His once long-dormant and compliant mind had been taken over by a new, stronger form. His passion had spurred him on, and he was feeling better by the second. Even Mamie Simon's threats weren't bothersome.

"Now, Madam," he persisted, "again, I shall leave you, and I am glad to do it. I have spoken my mind. And if I am not much mistaken, Mrs. Cratchit has a delicious mug of holiday eggnog with a dash of nutmeg waiting for me at home. . . . So, Merry Christmas to you, and good-day."

Tipping his hat and half-smiling at her with a sort of crooked grin, which was full of his natural warmth, he took another step backwards, trodding in the most worn and tattered pair of brown leather shoes one could ever find—with such large holes in the soles, too. His feet were barely protected from the slightest chill or dampness the earth or the stone floor might serve up. Nonetheless, with a small whoop and a "good-bye," he spun around lightly and happily on those old shoes and made his way towards the arched wooden door along the dark worn path in the concrete. He even began to whistle "Silent Night" before changing over to "Rudolph," feeling especially Christmassy with the lively tune in his bouncy feet.

Mamie Simon's now bloodshot eyes glowered with rage at the buoyant demeanor of her subordinate. How dare he! He had wished her Merry Christmas! He had even perpetrated some sort of light-footed dance right in the middle of her chamber! She was aghast at his Christian cheer and enthusiasm. She wanted to shout after the ragged man:

"Bah! Christmas and eggnog are humbugs! Mistletoe is a sham! Christmastime is for the happy and foolish!"

This type of outburst was, of course, her natural inclination towards another—but she did not do it. She held her tongue completely. Rather, there was a sudden and dramatic change in her demeanor in the opposite direction for the simple reason she had hatched a new scheme. Unbeknownst to Bob Cratchit as he reached the door, the transformation had occurred. As quickly as the lady glowered with rage, she softened in the other way. It was as if she'd become a compassionate and forgiving human in the wheezing of a breath. Her blinking eyes smiled and turned friendlier and her lips puckered like in a kiss. She even pinched her cheeks hoping to bring up some color from the depths. Then she stretched a single hand towards him as if to pull him back in a gentle, ladylike manner.

"My dear Cratchit, *please, please* stop," she begged. "I have been rough with you, too rough. Please do not go, my fair servant. Do not despair me. I must ask you to rethink this decision." She spoke more softly than ever before, hoping such a polite and friendly approach would change his mind. "Even though Christmas truly is a humbug."

He turned back to her, looking at her silently and skeptically from under the brim of his hat, his mussed hair falling in strands around his face and over his ears with his gloved hand ready to pull on the well-used cast-iron door handle. Christmas morning was drawing close. It would be upon the earth in less than twenty-four hours and he didn't want to spend another minute in this icy chamber—it was only a place to squander a life, to squander everything, because it could not be pretended away—and he wanted to whistle his way home.

"Oh, Cratchit," she went on, still the beggar, "I had you brainwashed for so long, for all of those years. Didn't you enjoy it?"

She tried smiling at him, to be affectionate with another soul for once in her life—aside from the souls of rats and ravens, of course!—but her opaque skin and the delicate muscles underneath would not comply.

"Enjoy the brainwashing?" he asked.

"Yes, yes, it was good, Cratchit, it was good. We have been a good team, you and I. I do believe you enjoyed being under my thumb. You can have my thumb again—I give it to you freely, sir. Yes, I will even give you new banker's books and many new pencils at your table and I will order the minions to rub your feet, too—they would be glad to do such a thing. As they rub, you can even kick their heads if it will entertain you." She directed a long index finger towards the suddenly dumbstruck minions kneeling on the stone floor. "I will feed you an extra bowl of gruel at lunchtime, if you please, and lower the rent on your little table and stool by the window. Yes, this will be very good, Cratchit. I will even give you tape to cover the holes in your shoes—oh, those poor shoes!—and I will have your old, moth-eaten sweaters and trousers mended with surplus cotton thread." She reached her arms towards him again, grasping at nothing, trying to look at him with caring, twinkling eyes. "I am not such a loathsome old wench, Cratchit, I assure you I am not. I will make you into a new man."

But her sincerity was insincere. As she leaned back, whatever charm and congeniality had swept over her was now disappearing like vapor into the air, and Bob Cratchit could tell. She couldn't keep up the facade as her haughty dreadfulness began returning to the surface. She tried smiling at him again, unsuccessfully, her contemptuous mouth and loose teeth encircled by thick red lipstick. In the lighting, her thin, distorted face seemed even more so, much like a depraved ferret. And her stern eyes and smugness showed through it all.

"I beseech you," she went on. "Do not fall into the embrace of Bitcoin, Bob Cratchit—you must not do it—it will not do you well. Oh, you may have dreams of glittering castles in the sky. You may have dreams of enchanted gatherings on tropical beaches. You may have all sorts of impossible visions. But I can assure you Bitcoin is a terrible glitch in the history of money . . . in history, period. Yes, my dear Cratchit, it is a curse against us *all*."

Of course, he did not believe her. He was already a new man and she was a conniver, steadfast in her mania. After so many years under her bitter gaze, he knew this without a doubt. And he could see it in her creased expression right now. She would never change because she did not know how to try, and he was all at once disgusted by every molecule that joined to make her into this relic.

"I promise you one thing, Mamie Simon," he replied with a smile in the face of it all, before she could spend another breath. "When it comes to Bitcoin, I am an elephant in my position—unmovable and unafraid. I will gore your reasoning with my tusks of sensibility." Having a gleam in his eyes and a shimmer to his cheeks, proud of his surprise performance so far—he had never been much of a talker—he grinned to himself. He was doing it after all of these years: He was standing up to her and firmly fighting for himself. No clergyman or politician could have used better words. He then added: "So keep talking, old lady, keep on talking. You'll soon be talking to yourself."

"Tut, tut!" she answered raspingly, changing her tone back to her natural state of meanness. Her eyes inside the caves stared out of their shadowy darkness. "Be smart for once, Cratchit, you grinning grunion. You've dug yourself into the sand with this Bitcoin nonsense. It's all a great hustle. Scandals and vandals to the core of it." She leaned towards him in her chair. "You must stay with me here at your little table by the window, *ser*vant, you must—I *command* you to do it! Your table is supported by four legs. Bitcoin is supported by *nothing*. Indeed, your own personal Tank is a real thing with real intrinsic value. You must realize this deep down, Cratchit, because it is obvious. Your

Tank cares for you. It will always be here for you. You can trust your Tank im*plicit*ly. . . ."

Staring at her dubiously, Bob Cratchit stood dismayed at her wild, overdone words while swaying on his legs impatiently but saying nothing. She stared back at him in frustration, silently chewing her tongue while brooding over this unexpected and difficult matter.

But it was clear she was moving along a track and not about to give in, and she pressed on:

"If you stay, Cratchit, I will even give Tiny Tim a new crutch, which you can return to me once he is dead and gone. I will be like a second mother to him until that day, if I have the time. Yes, I will even invite him to dine with me on my favorite imported foods of broiled steaks of polar bears and plates of succulent seal eyes and heaps of fried penguin wings—I'm told the penguins don't even miss their wings!" She clapped her hands together excitedly at such a prospect. Anything which lived on or near the ice was a favorite of hers. "So remain with me, Cratchit, as my daily servant and ledger man. These are my concessions. I beg you. There is far more for you here than Bitcoin will ever offer. Yes! You must stay right here with me for Bitcoin is a fraud, a hideous *fraud*."

She paused for a moment to catch her breath and wipe her lips and spray more perfume over her shoulders.

She was going at him now in the only way she knew how, reaching for any straw or fabrication she could use. To someone paying attention, they would have seen Bob Cratchit roll his eyes in disgust at so many of the absurdities manifesting from her brain. He then replied to her as succinctly and forthrightly, and as calmly, as he could:

"I daresay, old woman, Bitcoin is the opposite of a fraud."

"You *daresay*, Cratchit? No, *I* daresay! And I daresay Bitcoin *is* a fraud."

He shook his head and gave her a withering look. "On the contrary, Mamie Simon. Bitcoin is as much a cod as a fraud, if you would ever know the difference. Bitcoin is a currency and a protocol and a society and a universe unto itself—a virtual *parallel polis* alongside your unholy system—and most of all, it is a great promise to the future."

The high and mighty banker dismissed his words by raising her chin and turning her face away from him. "Oh, Cratchit, *humpf*—ridiculousness."

"Bitcoin brings certainty to an uncertain world," he added. "Without Bitcoin, everything ahead of us is dire. . . ."

He considered for a moment this small, wizened lady on the throne and her self-perpetuating financial scam against the world. She unwittingly sat at the top of an ever-wobbly Jenga tower lording over a game that kept so many wicked people in power but which move by move was growing unsteadier. He could only smile at the old hag because she simply could not see what was coming straight at her. She could not see the purity and elegance of Bitcoin and its power and relentless drive. No antagonist put in its way would ever be able to stop it because Bitcoin is truth and truth kills evil. Indeed, Bitcoin lived by a code that would fundamentally change everything in its path. He was sure of it.

Like an animal caged its entire life, she began swaying in her chair restlessly. "Dire, Cratchit, dire? I say *liar*."

Bob Cratchit was again getting eager to end this conversation. It was going nowhere and serving no purpose and there was little more he could say. Even though Bitcoin was still a newcomer to the scene, it was a one-of-a-kind thing that appeared on earth at a most opportune time for humans. And he had pleaded its case as best he could. The old woman understood gold, of course—the precious metal had been around forever. But gold was merely a place marker. It had served its purpose for millennia as the one-dimensional precursor to Bitcoin. It was mainly a hard-to-use glob of ore, a shiny nuisance. Time and people were moving on from it—indeed, gold had become an antique to the modern brain. A brain runs on electricity, after all, why not its money? So the young and vibrant Bitcoin had quietly stepped into the void.

As for Bob Cratchit, he could only present these facts as they were: Gold was no longer golden. Yet he had no way of making the stubborn lady understand, even with wishful eyes. She was simply too far gone. There is no ghoul like a high ghoul, and the thin air revolving around her teetering head had become too much. So he only added, as a closing:

"Come to grips with it, madam, before the day you are carried to the churchyard without an audience and without a tear. Bitcoin is here. It is good. It might just be the greatest thing in the world."

He said these last things with great conviction as he remained standing by the door, his hand poised on the handle ready to pull it.

Even against all of the facts, however, it was clear Mamie Simon was not done with him. She had relied on him so much for her banking and business over the years, keeping the ledgers up to date and filled with numbers, she did not want to see him go. He was too important. Indeed, who would be her chief clerk? Who would sit each day crouched over the little table? Who better could she look down upon?

"Stay with me, Cratchit," she insisted, "and join me to plan more unrest for the masses so we may pilfer their wealth. I petition you to stay, my good fellow! A little chaos is good for the soul. It will be good for my business of Simon & Morgue, Ltd., too. . . . Yes! Remember what I always do, Cratchit? Do you remember? I pay a few dollars to my friends the collectivists—who don't like being individuals—to collect into their comforting groups and protest and shout rhyming slogans at the people who do like being individuals. Oh, what easy seductions! And what feelings! My trick never fails to keep them all busy so no one pays any attention to me."

She threw her head back in delight, her stiff, laughing mouth agape and her stained teeth displayed. It's been said feelings are not guides to reality, but Mamie Simon wasn't complaining—her manipulations always worked so perfectly.

"It's quite the dickens, wouldn't you say, Cratchit?" she went on. "All those rioters with clouds inside their heads growing angrier by the moment just to help me gain more power? Bless their little green hearts." For an instant, she put her hands high into the air as if praising the heavens. "And what grand entertainment it is," she said. "You can even join me at the window to watch the chanting mobs accomplishing nothing, masquerading as do-gooders, fighting to enslave themselves all in the name of something to do. Most certainly, Bob Cratchit, my servant, we will howl and hoot and clap together like a proud audience." She was absolutely gleeful for the moment, finding great satisfaction in her ploys against the population—a population that had always done exactly as it was told. She thought he should feel the same way, too. She was sure her old dead-and-gone partner, J.P. Morgue, would. And why not? Who needs reason and thoughtfulness when one can simply succumb to the unruly crowd's wild emotions? Then she added: "Oh, yes, Cratchit, it is very good to be at the top as an instigator—confusion flows down and money flows up!"

The ragged chief clerk and best employee, however, was not interested in taking part in any such dark schemes. They were shameful and useless. He knew, even as her masked mobs made trouble, angling for some ideal fight—trying to bring the great down to mediocre and the mediocre down to oblivion—they would always become weaker with each Bitcoin created for the world.

He shook his head. "Your dark heart pumps your dark blood, Mamie Simon. Someday soon the hungry beast you've created will come to eat *you*."

Yet her manner remained unrelenting and grotesque. "Oh, Cratchit, don't act surprised," she said, her voice in a gurgle. "You know as well as I know everybody is greedy like me. But not everybody is *successfully* greedy like me—that is the difference."

"Evil is a dangerous game," he replied.

"So is betrayal."

The solitary figure high on the chair tapped her bony fingertips together in front of her face as if scheming a new plan, all the while gazing downward at him. And she chuckled again from deep in her phlegmy chest.

As for Bob Cratchit, he understood things differently. He understood that the exercise of rational self-interest by individuals is imperative for a successful society. Call it a form of greed, if you like. But the world according to Mamie Simon was naturally awful and sickening and something to be exploited—yes, she was a mean one! She sought to violate others' sovereign rights to meet her own ends, even if only to make herself feel better for a minute or two. She used immorality as a tool, as if she was a savage remnant of the industrial revolution's Gilded Age when anything went. Without a doubt, she traveled far beyond simple self-interest. She went straight into wickedness.

The old girl then stated, in confirmation of everything: "The public is one to take from, not partake in. And so that is what I do, Cratchit. I only mean to control society for my own profit and purposes—to control *everybody* in society, from its monsters to its ministers. They're all equal under me." She grinned at him knowingly. "That is my sole mission as an anti-capitalist, you see, and I am passionate in my cause. Does that really mean I am so bad?"

"Yes, that's exactly what it means."

"Ha, ha, Bob Cratchit, you nonbeliever. Think what you think and be that as it may. Until I am eaten by the beast I will always enjoy stuffing my purse with the population's easy-gotten treasure.

Like so many others, Mamie Simon did her dirty work just under the turbulent waves of society where prying eyes quickly become too distracted by the froth and commotion of the perpetual storm. She'd gotten richer every day because of it—yet never grew less morose—and she was not about to change her course.

All the same, Bob Cratchit was really only interested in Bitcoin and Liberty. To him, they were synonymous ideas and he could not understand why anybody would fight against them. Why shouldn't individuals control their own wealth? Their own destinies? Aren't *they* their own best advocates? Why should people continue forking over billions to rent-seeking bankers in the mere name of convenience? Why fund their gleaming skyscrapers and mahogany offices? Why fund their towering thrones and fancy colognes? Truly, why use banks at all?

For Bob Cratchit, the happiness of generations to come was surely in the balance and he became reflective, even melancholy, thinking about it all.

"I remember so many times while sitting here in this chamber," he said to her, gesturing towards the little stool and table, "asking myself the question: 'Who is Mamie Simon *really*?' I would ask the question because I never understood your dark ways." He shook his head gravely. "Then I would wonder about you more: Where does the darkness come from and why do you keep it? Why do you endlessly rail against the individual good? Why so much scorn? Why so much rapacity? On some days I wondered if you were pure evil or merely in need of a nap. But I finally realized I'd been overthinking these questions. To the extent it matters, I now understand."

"Is that so, Cratchit?" she asked in a growl. She tapped her front teeth with her long purple fingernails. "And *what* do you understand, pray tell?"

"It is really quite easy. I understand tyranny is only good for the tyrant. I understand Mamie Simon has tyrannized the world from her place of power to swindle and cheat to gain the wealth she has. And I understand she has no shame for any of it." He smirked. "Your mind, Mamie Simon, was born as simple and shallow as that. It is true: Evil lives in the shallows as easily as the depths."

"Bah! *Cratchit....*" she started to reply in the same growl, but she stopped herself short.

"This is why I will not take even the smallest and most innocent part in any more of your devilish doings," he continued. "While you and the ghost of your old dead-as-a-doornail partner—J.P. Morgue—destroy the world by pilfering its wealth, picking pockets like common street thieves, and conspiring to leave the population as poor as church mice, Bitcoin promises to save us all. That is why you hate it, isn't that so, old woman? Bitcoin is the solution to the hidden corruptors. Bitcoin is the solution to *you.*"

Mamie Simon only laughed in a small, weak manner at his blunt words. It was a forced laugh, as if she could see the veil hiding her immense power and dishonesty was slowly being lifted, if only to him. She had always lived in her money, like it was oxygen to her flesh, and now it had come to this. She had nothing more to say, so he went on undeterred with great faith in himself and his notions:

"Misery is your province, surrounding you like a dark army," he stated. "Most assuredly, I look forward to the day when Bitcoin will take you down, when it will charge right into this chamber like some latter-day Byzantine general fresh from the field and muscle you from that gaudy throne and tear your fraudulent money system apart. Sure, you can try to stop Bitcoin. You can try to stop the unstoppable. But it will be your last act—your downfall—Mamie Simon, if only because you don't understand the changing world it leads. You deny Bitcoin's great strengths: Its openness, its resilience against the controlling powers, how it is unbridled by human motivations, its strong worldwide ledger, the hard-money of it, the incorruptible and non-reversible transactions, the scarcity, the divisibility, the keepability . . . the *survivability*. And, like Christmas, Bitcoin is borderless. All of it together is an amazing dream: I say it is the dream of a thousand years. For, in the end, Bitcoin gives us separation of money and state and therefore freedom because, self-evident as it is, freedom doesn't come from the top." He paused briefly to gather himself, savoring the moment, before grinning at her calmly. "It's a great war now, old lady, the Bitcoiners versus you, and you have only slander as a weapon. So live in the matrix you created. I will live with Bitcoin." He raised an index finger into the air to make his point. "And with that, Mamie Simon, I say long live good sense, sound money, and Bitcoin capitalism."

Bob Cratchit pulled on the door, which squeaked and moaned on its iron hinges as you'd expect from a heavy wooden door of its age, and he stepped into the threshold of the archway. He smiled again briefly, to himself. The door and the threshold had seen plenty of sad people pass by and through them over the decades. Today, however, it would be a rare opposite experience for both.

He buttoned his frayed coat up to the top of his neck, preparing to depart, also wrapping an old scarf around his neck and shoulders—feeling the warmth. He was content. He had said what he could say and he could say no more. His derring-do had paid off, if only for himself.

Sadly for her, Mamie Simon's brain had long ago been locked into an immovable position not to be budged by anyone. There was no freshness or flexibility to it. It was a slow brain in a fast lane and it only did what it had always done. In fact, all of Bob Cratchit's words on this day had merely swirled around her silver head but never really entered. Not a single new thought or idea could find room for itself in there, and she was oblivious to this fact—and distraught for it.

Her non-laughing voice rose an octave seeing him about to exit and she cried out for him. She hated the fact someone in her banking tower had awoken to some new reality and was leaving because of it. The first sentence in Simon & Morgue's mission statement was "To Transform Each Employee into a Company Idiot"—and she had failed with him at this core value.

"No! Consider me, now, Cratchit. Consider *me*," she screamed. "With freedom and prosperity around the world I will lose power over the people. You know this, don't you? Freedom for the world is dangerous to people like me with our gold sacks. Think of me and my gang of busy bankers. We cannot let the unwashed commoners with all that dirt behind their ears use money we cannot create and control as we want. Where is the sense, Bob Cratchit? *Where is the sense?*" To her, the filthy populace could be allowed to rise only so far—to have only enough to be on the verge of pitiable. Such a result was always easy, too, because central banks—and *all* banks—are merely blinds for dastardly doings. She then scratched down the length of her neck in a long raking motion with one hand, as if attacking herself for spite, while wiping the back of her other hand across her now foaming mouth as her eyes became wilder and her voice rose higher. She was a poor example of the gentler persuasion as she pressed on: "The surplus population on the earth needs me and my bank to govern them," she declared. "I am sure of it, Cratchit. Surely you know this because you are one of them. Oh, the teeming surplus is chaotic rubbish without me, even if they don't know me or know I exist. . . ."

She was traveling on a course from Desperation to Delusion and gaining speed. She raised a single hand high above her head as her screeching continued. Her long, curled fingers and sharp fingernails on the hand formed a veritable eagle's claw.

"Bob Cratchit," she carried on in her high-pitched, rasping voice, "as I live and breathe, the people need my invisible hand for guidance. Look around you at the rudderless throng. Look at their despicable lives. Then look at my hand! They *need* it. They *deserve* it. It is their comforter. Don't you understand?"

Bob Cratchit did understand, and that was why he had become a Bitcoiner. Her sharp, crooked talon piercing the air was the opposite of freedom. It was an iron claw of oppression, each finger a rapier to be used to gore the innocent.

He quietly shook his head at her in disappointment, at her hubris and ego and everything else.

Mamie Simon could now see the battle had slipped away. It was over. But, even so, she wasn't going to give up yet. She put into the air her other arm, in exasperation, now clenching both fists above her head. "No, no, no, Cratchit," she cried in futility as she raised her eyes to the pointed ceiling. The circle of gargoyles high above, those lofty onlookers sitting on their tiny ledges, looked down on her in stony disappointment. "Stay with me in this high tower, Bob Cratchit," she implored. "Do not make your mind a Bitcoin prison. Do not catch the hideous fever. Do not do it! You piggy bankers will *never* dethrone the central bankers. Their gluttony has made them immovable. You *must* understand this. So stay seated at your Tank right here within these walls. *Be* with your Tank. *Love* your Tank. Your little Tank *needs* you."

She then pounded her fists onto the arms of the giant chair in hysterical frustration, screeching his name over and over: "Cratchit! Cratchit! Cratchit! . . . Oh, *Cratchit*. . . ."

But Bob Cratchit was still unmoved. He found her performance to be weak and pathetic and he nearly laughed to her over-painted face. Indeed, the way she beat upon the chair was the way she beat upon the world.

He merely shook his head and chuckled to himself from the doorway. "Ha, ha. Oligarchs are so temperamental."

He could clearly see her end would be coming, fast and efficient. It was obvious and inevitable and he didn't want to be there for it. Bitcoin would one day swallow the entire fiat system, and it already seemed to be swallowing her.

"This is how you want to be remembered?" he then asked, almost as an afterthought, once her bawling had dissipated and her head had slumped to her chest in a sort of emotional exhaustion. "The Scrooge of Bitcoin? An unhinged thief throwing spears at the winds of change? You are free to come to your senses at any time, Mamie Simon, to understand the wind serves great purposes all over the earth and can never be stopped."

"Humbug to it all, Cratchit," she moaned breathlessly, slowly lifting her gaze to him. "The wind is dangerous."

Her heavy head drooped again to her chest and hovered there limply like a wilting weed as her sad, empty eyes became glazed and watery under her shadowy brow, staring into nothingness. She was as much a fish as a fishwife. At the same time, her open lips hung wet with fresh drool which trickled in long strands onto the front of her colorful gown. Amongst the ruins, she whispered woefully to herself about things like recklessness and bleakness and "the rabies of magic money."

She seemed to have entered a final, irreversible state of being. It was not superficial and it was not contradictory. For Bob Cratchit, though, it was all the same.

"Once again, Mamie Simon, good-bye," he remarked from his place at the threshold as her lifeless eyes slid over to focus on him. "I will now gladly leave you to your rantings and ramblings. I will leave you to your barren greatness. I will leave you to your cries and moans and whinings, all of it, old lady, because I am doing no good in bringing you around. The Bitcoin Ideal can surely save you. I only fear you'll catch on when your chance is gone." He made a quarter-turn towards the door. "At any rate, I must go. I am a better man beyond these thick corporate walls. And I look forward to being at home tonight with my family singing carols after dinner and telling happy stories over a steaming bowl of Christmas Eve pudding." He gently tipped his hat again, and added with a satisfied grin: "So, God be with you forever, Mamie Simon. I am going out into the world to my better prospects—and to spread the message about the great dimensions of Bitcoin . . . the hashrates and the halvings and the hodlings and—"

"Oh, yes, Cratchit," she interrupted suddenly, her head rising. She wiped her red-coated lips with the back of her dry, bony hand, speaking to him all at once with a new sense of vigor as if the argument had come back to life. "I am quite aware of *those* things. I have a mind to write a great book someday, *The Twaddle of the Hodl*, to show the world point by point how Bitcoin is a fraud. You'll see, Cratchit. I just need more time to come up with good reasons why."

At this moment, still kneeling at her feet, the minions stopped massaging Mamie Simon's toes and ankles and heels, even her fallen arches, and they rose from the hard floor with looks of renewal and understanding on their faces. They had been listening to the quarrel and whispering intently among themselves. Now, they seemed to have made up their minds about something.

To be sure—taking a look back in time—the minions had not many years heretofore been innocent children, strong and happy and free, unpolluted by the urgings and "studies" of their dishonorable schools and every one of those others along the way with secret agendas of control and conformity. From their earliest classrooms, they had been taught the world was mean and bad and out to get them, that they should always worry. "Be afraid," they were told. "Afraid of what?" they would ask. "Everything," was always the answer.

Not knowing any better, they had bowed at the Altar of Anxiety.

And now they were here, given over to the similar powers of Mamie Simon—and to look at them! The entire group of minions was a beaten-down morass of frowns. A smile was as foreign as a kindly word. Sorrow was as common as the cold air. All of them were weak, shivering, diminutive husks of young adults because the sky was always falling. Day-to-day a black cloud of stress hung over their heads until the long-off prospects of arthritis, dementia, and death in a nursing home became happy thoughts—and their downtrodden state of affairs gave Mamie Simon great joy.

Yet, suddenly, there was a palpable sea change in each of them.

"Minions!" Mamie Simon declared, a strained look of disbelief on her face. She wondered what sort of mass occurrence was happening right in front of her. Her shrill, alarmed voice reverberated in the stone chamber as she gravely pointed multiple fingers at the rogue band of company idiots. Her teeth swayed and clinked in her excitement. "Return to my feet, minions—and finish the important work you started!"

But the strangest thing happened instead. . . .

The minions did not go back to kneel in front of her throne. They did not so much as make a twitch in her direction. Rather, in unison, they silently turned and walked over to Bob Cratchit by the door and stood closely around him, their shoulders thrown back straight and strong—as though they had taken back their inherent strength—appearing as defiant as he did. He hadn't withdrawn all the way from the chamber yet, and he was glad. Realizing what was happening, looking from face to face, he stepped in and smiled at them all. The minions looked back at him in amazement.

For Mamie Simon, though, this group reaction might've been the biggest insult of her life, a real "humbugger" as some would later say. She was stunned at the outright mutiny. She looked as if someone had run her through with a sword—pale and impaled. Her bad ways were being rejected and she started to panic. Even these seemingly flat, wonderless minions were thinking freely now.

"Bah! Heed me, minions, if you ever want to see a tiny raise or a modest promotion here in this tall tower," the shoeless old lady went on as her toes wiggled in their autonomy. "Listen to me, minions, you must! You are in my presence. I have grace. I have majesty. I am a grand banker, a jumbo banker—an *alpha* banker! I hold immense power and influence in the world. Indeed, I can pull a lever and make things happen." She pleaded like never before because she had never before pleaded—what a day it was!—and to plead with such lowly humans as *these*. But ha! She went on anyway: "*Look* at me! *See* me! I am charming. I sit on a throne. I have glimmering hair. My warts are fine . . . You must look my way."

Mamie Simon frantically peered to and fro at all of them, one to the next, considering her options. But her options were nil. Her screechings up until this point had been bearing no results, yet she continued aimlessly in disconnected emotional fits and starts and undigested thoughts in the only way she knew how, swaying in her chair:

"My minions! My comrades! *What is happening here?* What is *happening?* You must stay with the program. . . . Do what I and the globalists expect of you. Be the cowering pawns you were meant to be. . . . Sure the banking system is warped and wayward and fat with excess, but *so what?* It is *familiar*. . . . Don't you see this loving chamber is your destiny? Please put the pudding back in your knees. Put the curve back in your spines. Look here, I'll even give you each a penny jar! Yes, my good minions, come back to me, come right back here—don't force me to make you into a pack of saccharin-smiling bank tellers. Do you want *that?* No, of course not! So choose my *floor*, not the door—my *feet*, not the street. . . . Oh, fellow spirits, do not listen to Bob Cratchit. Do not run to Bitcoin. Surely Bitcoin is novel, surely it is scarce, but surely it is not *desirable*. . . . Please, please, my minions, I'm too big to fail. Say you're jesting! Tell me you're some kind of silly, misguided wisencoiners on a Gotham City lark. I *beg* you. . . . But tell me—*where is all of this going?*"

She suddenly started kicking her bare heels in rapid succession against the front of her throne in juvenile frustration. "No, no, no!" she carried on. "Don't listen to him, minions—*not Cratchit.*" Then she carelessly threw a handful of paper money into the air and wildly tossed her hands into the air, too, shrieking about the ferocious dangers of volition and imagination.

Even though Mamie Simon made breakdowns look easy, the minions were hardly impressed—as she blathered on even more:

"If you won't attend to my feet then go down to your desks and manipulate the markets. Buy more silver bars. Short Bitcoin, if you have to. Do *something* to fill my coffers. . . ."

None in the group, however, obeyed her commands. They hardly turned an ear, in fact, as her voice trailed off into the chamber's heavy air. Rather, they began calmly revealing their new thoughts among themselves.

"I want to own some Bitcoin," one of the young minions said to the others.

"Yes, liberty and decentralization seem to be the future of things," another stated.

"I like the ideas of free-will and self-reliance and individualism," still another added.

"Now I see I've been living in a banker's fog," a fourth joined in, taking off his glasses and wiping the lenses. "In the Ivies and here I've been toeing the line as a robotic machine espousing all kinds of other people's bad ideas, but now it's clear I've been wrong. I'm not one to stay brainwashed. I'm not an angry same-thinker in the crowd. I'm a real person who can change his mind. I can even be happy and optimistic. In fact, I'm free to go my way!"

A fifth, a plump, rosy-cheeked minion with her hair in pigtails, chimed in saying, "I'm tired of feet," to which they all clapped and cheered.

All of the minions next began to wipe their hands, to clean them of the smell of feet. They shook each others' hands in congratulations, also, and shook the hands of Bob Cratchit and patted his back and crowded around him and told him he made more sense to them than anyone they'd ever heard, especially while at their greedy, deceitful, bereft-of-common-sense universities.

For Bob Cratchit's part, he was immensely proud of them—and he said so. They had each decided to leap forward and try something new and unknown, to favor themselves, to be freethinkers and self-determining individuals beyond the forces of any group as, in fact, they existed for their own sakes. None would get back their wasted time, but they were able to take back their personal powers and healthfulness and good postures. Indeed, they were seizing control of their lives on the earth beyond the monolithic racket.

What a change in outlook!

He even addressed his earlier criticisms of them. The criticisms needed to be stated, according to him, in order to jolt their senses—to let them start seeing things as they really were, to set them on a path to enlightenment—which the now-former minions understood perfectly since all of what he had said was true.

His eyes sparkled like morning sunshine on a frosty window as he declared with a smile, "Rejoice, my good friends. You are living on this wonderful Earth. And you are young and alive during The Age of Bitcoin!"

Certainly, this newly formed group was in marvelous spirits. And through all of it, as they gathered and talked and squeezed each other's shoulders and clapped each other's backs, happy in their minds and no longer conflicted in their souls—and with Bitcoin on their tongues!—Bob Cratchit stood among them beaming with a conqueror's expression on his face, one that said:

"Today the minions, tomorrow the world!"

The result was not the same for Mamie Simon, however, who was barely hanging on. The old bird now sat perched all alone on her throne wringing her hands in anguish—her thoughts a din of quivering voices—mumbling over and over to herself, "Bitcoin is a fraud! Bitcoin is a fraud!" As she did so, her murky blue eyes darted here and there as if searching her own stale mind for something meaningful, perhaps a solution to her dishonest and Scrooge-like ways, but finding nothing.

In the meantime, all of the one-time minions and their new mentor, still chatting and giggling among themselves, each smiling and bouncing with lightness in their steps, began to leave the chamber. Never had there been seen such a happy and gregarious batch of laddies and lassies as this inside the tower. If one understands the reference, they were as happy as old Fezziwig on the dance floor. As a result, the chamber had a different look and feel to it. It was like something good and mysterious had been launched into the place—the air suddenly seemed warmer and the stone walls less cold and gray. A slim beam of new sunlight had even split the clouds and come in through the window. One might've expected the mournful fireplace to simply burst into dancing orange flames.

Alas, none of this fellowship and well-being made its way to Mamie Simon. She was about to be left by herself and she did not give in to it quietly. Afraid of the loneliness soon to come into her life—her ornate throne and the green feather boa would make poor company—she pressed her hands to the sides of her head for an instant and then reached out with them and wailed after the happy party like she was a ghost in despair:

"But minions! My feet! My jowls! *Please* do not abandon me. Who will run my investments? Who will help conspire with the central bankers? Who will explain fractional-reserve lending to me?"

But they did not listen to her. They did not react in any way. They didn't look back to see her shakily take a drink from the tall goblet at her side as some of the black liquid escaped from one corner of her sad mouth and streamed like a river down her chin and onto her bright gown. They didn't see her slump in despair or pull at her hair or messily apply a fresh coat of trembling red lipstick to her mouth to help her feel better about herself. Her former stooges didn't so much as take a glance backwards, in fact, when her echoing wail transformed into a hollow, pathetic whimper as if she was melting straight-away into her overgrown chair. They simply closed the door behind themselves, talking and celebrating in their camaraderie. They even strolled past two stiff, imposing guards standing outside the doorway—who each might've smiled knowingly at hearing the word "Bitcoin"—as the entire group agreed, jovially, to bundle up and go down to the snowy streets of Gotham City to sing some Christmas carols and jingle some bells and tell everybody they encountered about "the Great Bitcoin." Bob Cratchit gladly offered to toast each of his new friends afterward—for it was still early in the day—with "a Christmas cup of mead and a sweet pastry" in celebration, each of them wholeheartedly approving.

And he was as good as his word.

As it turned out, this particular Christmas season—and every Christmas season that followed—was a most-merry time for Bob Cratchit and his family at home. He acquired the largest goose in the butcher's window for each Christmas dinner. Carols were sung. Church bells rang. And Tiny Tim, always so well-behaved, became a healthy and hearty little boy getting the attention he needed, happy to retire his crutch to the far corner of his bedroom. His father no longer even had any need to carry him on his shoulder, as was his custom, although he sometimes did out of endearment. In their happiness, Bob Cratchit and Tiny Tim and the whole Cratchit family walked leisurely through the many tinseled shops with music in the air and bought all sorts of Christmas toys and presents each year for themselves and friends and charities with the little pieces of Bitcoins they earned and saved. There was no doubt they kept Christmas in their hearts and Bitcoin in their wallets. These were amazing times.

Meanwhile, as the months and years went by, poor Mamie Simon's brain transformed into an ossified clump and she was soon forgotten by everyone. Her financial business of fraud and deception and general disagreeableness had failed miserably. Her throne was sold at auction and her once pretty clothes and shiny hair became dull and out of date and her neglected feet turned into dry, gnarled stumps. Even the few government coins and paper bills she kept tucked away deep in her raggedy purse became worthless and nothing more than common museum pieces. Indeed, Mamie Simon's deliverance was complete. She spent the rest of her life disheveled and alone wandering the backstreets and littered parks of Gotham City, muttering wild and incoherent lamentations—"Oh, J.P. Morgue, my old partner," she would cry without answer, "come back to help me, come back whether you're a ghost in chains or not!"—eventually wearing nothing but old burlap sacks over her stooped shoulders while leaving a trail of her rotted brown and yellow teeth on the ground.

If only she had purchased some Bitcoin.

For, as it eventually came to be, Bitcoin's grand prophecy was fulfilled: It was an incredible success. From one Christmas to the next Bitcoin believers across the earth reveled in the glorious new freedom and prosperity it provided, happy that overbearing centralized governments and so many fiendish, powerful people in the old corrupt system had been defeated—Evil and Ignorance and Want were on the run. Christmas is about joyous celebrations around love and kindness and abundance, after all, not about wrecking lives.

And guess what! In the end, as Tiny Tim said to his family over a cup of eggnog on that wonderful Christmas morning next to the decorated tree, and as he said on every Christmas morning that followed, "God bless us, everyone, for this is the way it always should be. . . ."

About the Author

Paul W. Samuelson is an indie author currently working on several new writing projects, including the third book in his middle-grade space adventure series *The Boys of Earth-180*. Paul grew up in Minot, North Dakota and he lives in Boise, Idaho. Please leave your review of *The Scrooge of Bitcoin* on Amazon—it will be appreciated.

Printed in Great Britain
by Amazon